From Trash to Treasure

By Liza Alexander
Illustrated by Joe Ewers

A GOLDEN BOOK • NEW YORK

Published by Golden Books Publishing Company, Inc.,
in conjunction with Children's Television Workshop

A portion of the money you pay for this book goes to Children's Television Workshop. It is put right back into SESAME STREET and other CTW educational projects. Thanks for helping!

On Sesame Street every day of the week is recycling day! On Monday Ernie bundles old newspapers and ties them with string. Bert hauls the bundles to the curb for the recycling truck to pick up.

"New things can be made from trash," Bert explains proudly. "We don't like to waste, so we recycle!"

"Hey, Ernie and Bert!" calls Oscar. "Check out our trash treasures."

It's a party! Lots of little grouches are using old newspaper to make hats, airplanes, and kites.

"We grouches were the first recyclers because we love trash," Oscar explains. "But we recycle the grouch way—we keep our trash and use it again! See? We turn trash into treasure. Heh-heh-heh!"

On Tuesday Elmo's mommy brings home used paper from the office. Elmo draws pictures on the back of the paper. Elmo knows that saving paper saves trees.

"Look!" says Elmo. "Elmo made a tree. Elmo loves, loves, loves trees!"

Filthomena, a little grouch, loves to color, too. But Filthomena doesn't color on the back of the paper. She colors over the writing on the front! Filthomena makes a beautiful scribble-scrabble. "Trash to treasure," she says. "That's the grouch way!"

On Wednesday little monsters flatten out empty cardboard boxes so they can be recycled. "Cardboard is made of paper, too," says a little monster. "Old cardboard can be made into new cardboard!"

Little grouches keep empty cartons and use them for blocks. "We're building a beautiful city of trash!" says Filthomena. "Trash to treasure! Hee-hee-hee!"

On Thursday the Count and Countess return empty bottles and cans to Hooper's Store. First they count the empties. Then they count the money!

"Wonderful! Forty-one bottles and cans!" says the Count. "We get two dollars and five cents back! Thank you, Cookie Monster."

Oscar keeps empty bottles and cans and turns them
into musical instruments. Outside the store Oscar's Tin
Can Grouch Band gives a concert. What a ruckus!

"All right!" yells Oscar. "Play it! Trash to treasure.
That's the grouch way!"

On Friday Prairie Dawn collects her aluminum cans and plastic bottles. Then she sorts empty glass bottles and jars into different crates. There's one crate for clear glass, one for green, and one for brown. "Old glass can be cleaned and used again," says Prairie Dawn. "This is an excellent way to recycle!"

But why is Prairie Dawn saving old bottle caps?

Prairie Dawn saves bottle caps so she can give them to Grundgetta! Grundgetta uses the bottle caps to make jewelry.

"Trash to treasure," says Grundgetta. "That's the grouch way!"

On Saturday Big Bird gives clothes he has outgrown to Little Bird.

Granny Bird uses worn-out clothes to make something new. She cuts the scraps into patches and sews the patches into a beautiful quilt.

Grundgetta likes old clothes because they look great with her bottle cap jewelry. "Trash to treasure," says Grundgetta. "That's the grouch way!"

On Saturday afternoon Telly is fixing a broken toaster at the Fix-It Shop. "Soon this toaster will be good as new," says Telly. "I bet it will make perfect toast!"

Oscar has a broken toaster, too. "This old toaster makes perfectly burned toast," says Oscar, "so I'll keep it and use it again. That's the grouch way! Heh-heh-heh!"

On Sunday everybody brings their trash to the recycling drive. Nobody on Sesame Street likes to waste, and everybody knows that old things can be used to make new things. Everybody pitches in!

But where are all the grouches?

Here are the grouches!

"Trash to treasure," says Oscar. "That's the grouch way. Heh-heh-heh! And don't forget—don't litter!"